DANDELION'S Vanishing Vegetable Garden

For a free color catalog describing Gareth Stevens' list of high-quality books, call 1-800-341-3569 (USA) or 1-800-461-9120 (Canada).

Beechwood Bunny Tales
Aunt Zinnia and the Ogre
Dandelion's Vanishing Vegetable Garden
Family Moving Day
Mistletoe and the Baobab Tree
Periwinkle at the Full Moon Ball
Poppy's Dance
Violette's Daring Adventure

Library of Congress Cataloging-in-Publication Data

Huriet, Geneviève.
    [Jardin de Dentdelion Passiflore. English]
    Dandelion's vanishing vegetable garden / written by Geneviève Huriet ;
illustrated by Loïc Jouannigot.
        p.   cm. — (Beechwood bunny tales)
    Translation of: Le jardin de Dentdelion Passiflore.
    Summary: While the other Bellflower bunny children plant vegetables in their
garden, Dandelion decides to plant strawberries which soon become the target
of a hungry turtle.
    [1. Rabbits—Fiction. 2. Gardening—Fiction. 3. Turtles—Fiction.] I. Jouannigot,
Loïc, ill. II. Title. III. Series.
PZ7.H95657Dan   1991   [E]—dc20   90-46857
    ISBN 0-8368-0526-7 (lib. bdg.)
    ISBN 0-8368-1127-5 (trade)

North American edition first published in 1991 by
Gareth Stevens Publishing
1555 North RiverCenter Drive, Suite 201
Milwaukee, Wisconsin 53212, USA

English text by MaryLee Knowlton

Printed in the United States of America

2 3 4 5 6 7 8 9 98 97 96 95 94

BEECHWOOD BUNNY TALES

DANDELION'S
Vanishing
Vegetable Garden

written by GENEVIÈVE HURIET   illustrated by LOÏC JOUANNIGOT

Gareth Stevens Children's Books
MILWAUKEE

Spring had come to Beechwood Grove. Spring meant gardening, and the Bellflower bunnies loved to grow vegetables almost as much as they loved to eat them.

One day, Papa Bramble called his children out to the garden. "Your plots are ready," he said. "You can sow your seeds!"

Periwinkle, Violette, Poppy, and Mistletoe grabbed their gardening tools and went to work. "You, too, Dandelion," said Papa. "This year you're big enough for your own garden."

Dandy was speechless with joy. Papa led him to a sunny corner, sheltered by a stone wall. "This is your plot," he told Dandelion.

"What are you going to plant, Dandy?" asked Aunt Zinnia.

"Everything!" Dandy exclaimed. "Carrots, peas, beans, zucchini, peppers, broccoli . . ."

"Wait a minute, there!" laughed Papa. "You already have strawberry plants. Just sow a few rows of radishes and lettuce and a few rows of carrots and onions. That will be plenty for a first garden. Call me if you need help!"

"I can handle this myself," Dandelion thought. And he set to work with his shovel and watering can. The voices of the other bunnies swirled around him as he worked.

"Chop up those big chunks."

"Don't seed too close."

"Pull out those weeds."

"Don't overwater."

Dandy ignored them all.

That evening, the older bunnies followed Dandelion around
the house, offering unwanted advice.
"You should have weeded today."
"You gave your seeds too much water."
And from Mistletoe came the worst tease of all. "Maybe you
just want to grow weeds, Dandelion."

That was more than Dandelion could take. He flew across the room and grabbed Mistletoe by the shirt.

"Enough brawling!" Papa said sternly as he separated his angry children. "We are gardeners, not wrestlers. Give Dandelion a chance to learn on his own. When Grandpa comes in six weeks, he'll see what fine gardeners you are."

In the days that followed, the young gardeners were busy weeding, watering, pinching back, and thinning out. Soon, four of the gardens were bursting with lush green plants.

The fifth garden was Dandelion's. He had watered it so much that some plants had grown yellow and died. Eager to see his radishes grow, he had pulled up a few every day. They were all gone long before they were big enough to eat.

Dandy decided to sow his seeds again. This time, the older bunnies did not offer advice. But luckily for Dandelion, they did talk while they worked.

"Today I will weed the strawberries."
"No need to water today because of last night's rain."
Dandelion listened to their chatter and did as they did.
And his garden grew! The night before his grandpa's visit,
he looked over his garden with pride.

The radishes had big,
green leaves, and the
strawberries were ripening.
At the garden's entrance, he
had let a giant dandelion
grow so Grandpa would
know whose garden this was.

The next morning, Papa and Periwinkle left Beechwood Grove to meet Grandpa. Aunt Zinnia and the other bunnies stayed home to prepare for his welcome dinner.

When they finished, Mistletoe went out to play. As he passed Dandelion's garden, he saw something strange. "That silly Dandy has decorated his garden with a big, ugly stone," he thought.

But as Mistletoe watched, the "stone" stuck out four scaly paws, a tip of a tail, and a flat head. A turtle!

"Bah! Dandy can chase it away himself!" Mistletoe exclaimed, and off he went.

That left Tallulah, a turtle with exquisite taste in vegetables, in Dandelion's garden. Cautiously, she stretched out her paws and then her tail. Finally, she poked out her head and blinked her greedy, beady eyes.

"He's gone. Now I shall do brunch."

Much later, Dandelion came for one last look at his garden. Such a horror met his eyes! The dandelion had no flowers. The radishes had been trampled. Several heads of lettuce had been torn apart and thrown aside. And there in the middle of the strawberries, her eyes half-closed in delight, was Tallulah.

"You horrible, terrible thief!" Dandelion cried as Tallulah withdrew into her shell. "Come out, you coward!"

In a flash, Dandy turned her onto her back. There she was, helpless, you might think. Not Tallulah.

"You ruined my whole garden!" Dandy cried.

"Well, what do you expect, my boy? I am a turtle. Now stop that fussing. Don't you know I am a magician? I can make your garden even better than it was!"

"You can?" snuffled Dandelion. "Oh, please! Won't you?"

"I suppose I can," said crafty old Tallulah. "But you'll have to fetch me meadow herbs for my magic."

"I will! I will!" cried Dandy.

"But first, push me into the shade to wait, won't you?" Tallulah asked sweetly. Dandy pushed the turtle into the shadow against the wall. No sooner had he dashed off than Tallulah pushed herself against the wall and rocked herself upright in a moment.

"I didn't live ninety years being outsmarted by bunnies," said Tallulah as she laughed a low, mean turtle laugh and toddled off.

When Dandelion returned, he looked high and low for Tallulah.
"I've been so foolish," he sighed, looking at his ruined garden.
He sadly picked up his rag bunny. In a dark corner of the toolshed,
he curled up on an old potato sack and cried himself to sleep.

By this time, Papa and Periwinkle had returned with Grandpa. The bunnies led Grandpa straight to their gardens. As they reached Dandy's plot, Grandpa knew at once what had happened. "A turtle has had a feast here," he said. "Poor Dandy!"

Just then, the family noticed that Dandy wasn't there. Everyone began to search, especially Mistletoe, who felt terrible about his morning meanness.

"I've found him," he called from the toolshed. Dandelion awoke in Papa's arms and told his sad story.

"It sounds like Tallulah," sighed Grandpa. "I've lost more than one crop to her myself."

No one felt any need to tease or laugh, not even Mistletoe.

Once again, Dandy's garden needed to be replanted. This time, everyone helped.

"We've nearly got this garden back in shape — and just in time for dinner!" said Aunt Zinnia.

The dinner! Dandelion had forgotten all about it. "No nasty old turtle will spoil Grandpa's welcome dinner!" he laughed. He handed Mistletoe one paw of his rag bunny, and together they all went home.